3/22/01

THE LITTLE NED STORIES

Book One

Written by

Edward Allan Faine

Illustrated by

Joan C. Waites

To Katlyn:
Hope you enjoy the
book.

IM Press

First Printing 1999
Manufactured in the United States of America

IM Press
P.O. Box 5346
Takoma Park, Maryland 20913-5346
301-587-1202

Cover design by Joan C. Waites.
All rights reserved by artist.

These stories appeared in different form in *Prolific Writers Magazine*, *Rockford Review* and *Slice of Life*.

Library of Congress Cataloging-in-Publication Data
Faine, Edward Allan, 1937-
   Little Ned stories / written by Edward Allan Faine ; illustrated by Joan C. Waites.
     p.   cm.
   "Book one."
   Summary: Three seperate stories describe the experiences of a six-year-old boy living in West Virginia in the 1950s.
   ISBN 0-9654651-5-2   (pbk.)
   [1. Family life--West Virginia--Fiction. 2. Halloween--Fiction.
3. Fear--Fiction. 4. West Virginia--Fiction.] I. Waites, Joan C.,
i11. II. Title.
PZ7.F1436L1   1999
[Fic]--dc21   98-52047
                                                             CIP
                                                              AC

See last page 128 for ordering and other information.

DEDICATION

NO SOAP

To Little Boys And Trucks

THE BOY WHO HATED HALLOWEEN

To Halloweens Past

THE OCEAN VACATION

To The Big Blue Endless Ocean

NO SOAP

NOTE TO BOYS AND GIRLS, MOMMIES AND DADDIES AND EVERYBODY

NO SOAP is a colloquial expression, meaning—take your pick—NO WAY, NO DICE, NO HOPE, maybe even NOPE. While rarely used today, the phrase NO SOAP was a common expression in the United States in the first half of the twentieth century, as common as BEES KNEES and CATS PAJAMAS.

On occasion, NO SOAP can still be heard today by little boys in trucks on the dusty, bumpy-clunky backroads of Appalachia; especially, on the hilly, pine-edged, back-country trails that wend their way through the heavenly State of West Virginia.

CONTENTS

Wow! Look at all these chapters, boys and girls, just like a big grownup book, ain't it?

1. MR. JENKINS' TRUCK

I loved riding with Mr. Jenkins in
his truck. I got to see all kinds of
neat stuff and meet lots of nice
people. I was the only six-year-
old boy in Belle, West Virginia who
rode in his truck.

Mr. Jenkins let me drive, too!

I turned the key to start the motor and helped him push the gear stick back and forth.

When we were on a straight road, I'd put my hand on the steering wheel next to his and help him steer.

He warned me, "Little Ned, don't you tell your mother I let you drive my truck, you hear."

And I never did.

2. MR. JENKINS' MOVIE HOUSE

Mr. Jenkins was building a moving picture house. Everybody in town wanted to know when it would be finished.

Mr. Jenkins would tell them, "As soon as Little Ned and I get it done, we'll let you know.

"Save up your dollars. It's gonna open soon."

Farley, Clarence and I helped Mr. Jenkins build the movie house.

I'd go in his truck and help him load the bags of nails, the lumber boards, and the cement bags, while Farley banged the nails in the boards and Clarence stirred the cement.

Like everybody else, I couldn't wait until it was finished.

Mr. Jenkins said I could see the very first picture show for free, and bring Mother and Daddy, too.

3. OUR HOUSE

Mr. Jenkins came by our house almost every day after breakfast.

He'd stand by the screen door with his big straw hat in his hand and his pipe put away in his pocket so's Mother couldn't see it.

Mother didn't let him in the house because he had mud and squishy spiders on his boots.

One day, Mr. Jenkins came by and said what he always said, "How's my Little Ned? You ready for a hard day's work?"

Mother butted in. "Let's ask Mr. Jenkins if you can go first. We don't want to be imposin' now."

Mr. Jenkins stood up for me like he always did. "No Ma'am, he never gets in my way. I gets twice as much work done when he's helpin'."

"Go on then," she turned to me, "You be a good boy now, Little Ned. Here, take your peanut butter and grape jelly sandwich. And wipe your mouth when you're done eating."

4. FIND THE MAN WITH THE $ MONEY $

I climbed up in the cab of Mr. Jenkins' truck and sat on my special pillow so I could see out the windows.

Mr. Jenkins climbed in and, before we started the truck, he told me what we had to do.

"Today is a real important day. We got to get some money so we can finish the movie house.

"So, help me start the truck and we'll go up the road a piece and find the man with the money."

5. THE BLACKSMITH SHOP

We drove a long time and I had to help more than I usually did. My arm got tired steering the wheel, but I didn't say anything.

We stopped at the Blacksmith Shop and Mr. Jenkins went inside.

I waited in the truck and watched the horses munchy munch-munch their hay.

Finally, he came out shaking his head, jumped in the truck and said, "No soap. He's not here. But I know where we can find him.

"Let's go."

6. THE SAWMILL

We turned down a bumpy road. I let Mr. Jenkins do all the driving.

We stopped at a noisy sawmill—ZinnNNNGGGG, ZINGGGGG!

Mr. Jenkins went inside for a little bit and then came out and got right back in the truck.

"Well, he's not here, either.

"No soap again."

7. BACK TO THE MOVIE HOUSE

We went back to the movie house.

Mr. Jenkins yelled from the truck and Farley and Clarence came running.

After they talked awhile, Mr. Jenkins slid behind the steering wheel and slammed the door real hard. WHAM!

"Darn! No Soap. Let's go to the brickyard, we might find him there."

Off we went again.

8. THE BRICKYARD

By the time we got to the brickyard, I'd eaten half my sandwich. This time I got out of the truck and followed him all around. As we passed through the shed on the way back to the truck, Mr. Jenkins shook his head and muttered, "No soap."

He stopped, scratched his head, looked at me and said, "Okay, Little Ned, we got one last chance.

"The man with the money better be at the General Store. We gotta get that money if we're ever going to finish the movie house." So we headed for the General Store.

9. THE GENERAL STORE

Mr. Jenkins didn't talk much. He looked unhappy, like Daddy looked when I did something wrong. I'd never seen him unhappy before.

So when we came to the General Store, I opened the truck door, jumped down on the ground, and ran inside the store to find the man with the money.

Nobody was there except old Mister Peterson.

I went back outside and broke the bad news.

"No soap's not here either."

Mr. Jenkins laughed real hard, picked me up, swung me around and sat me down.

"Now what's that you say?

"*No soap's not here either.*"

Then he laughed again.

He put me in the truck and we went back to the movie house.

10. TO THE MOVIE HOUSE AGAIN

He told Farley and Clarence about me saying *no soap's not here either*.

They all laughed and bent over and slapped their knees. I didn't see what was so funny. How could we finish the movie house? We didn't find *No Soap* and we didn't get the money.

It was hard to understand big people sometimes. First they're happy, then they're not happy, and then they're happy again.

And you never know why.

11. BACK HOME

For the rest of the day they smiled and laughed and called me *No Soap* instead of Little Ned.

Then Mr. Jenkins took me home and told Mother the *No Soap* story through the screen door.

She laughed, too.

Big people just didn't make any sense.

12. THE NEXT MORNING

The next morning after breakfast Mr. Jenkins showed up at the screen door like he usually did. "How's my *No Soap* today?"

"Did you find the man with the money?" I asked.

"Sure did. And, by gosh and by golly, guess what? Would you believe, the man with the money—old Mister Peterson—was at the General Store yesterday afternoon when we were there. We just left too soon, that's all. Now we can finish the movie house."

"Oh, goody," I said.

13. MY NEW NICKNAME

"What do you think of your new nickname, *No Soap*?" Mother asked.

"It's okay," I said, smiling.

We had the money to finish the movie house and that made me happy.

From then on, everybody called me *No Soap*, and that was all right with me.

The other kids had names like Jimmy, Tom and Billy. But I had a nickname, like an Indian name, and that made me special.

THE BOY WHO HATED HALLOWEEN

CONTENTS

Hey, kids, get ready for the double ending.

You get to choose the ending you like best.

How about that!

1. AUNT BETTY'S HOUSE

"Come here," Mother said, pulling me close to her. "Let me rub charcoal on your face so you'll look like a bum."

"I don't wanna be a bum!" I said in a loud voice.

Mother knelt in front of me. "Little Ned! Look at me! You're six-years-old, going on seven.

"Show me you're a big boy. You'll have lots of fun at the Halloween party."

"I don't wanna go to the party, Mother," I whined. "I don't know anybody in Aunt Betty's town."

"You can make new friends at the Halloween party," Mother said.

"It's like a birthday party, only better. There'll be games and prizes. And you can bob for apples, and play pin-the-tail on the donkey."

"I don't wanna go!"

Mother plopped an old floppy hat on my head and told Aunt Betty, "We'll drop Little Ned at the church and then we'll go to the Coffee Shop and visit awhile."

2. THE HALLOWEEN PARTY

Mother left me at the church with Pastor Williams. He took me to this big room full of noisy kids and told me to go have fun.

There were a few kids my age, but most were older. Everybody was dressed in freaky costumes—ghosts, pirates, cowboys, dancers, and clowns—running around, yelling and screaming.

I went to the side of the room, slumped on a bench and stared at the floor.

Soon, the Wicked Witch of the West and Caspar the Ghost came over. The Wicked Witch asked, "What's your name?"

Before I could say anything, Caspar the Ghost repeated, "What's your name? I'll give you this candy apple if you tell me."

"I don't know," I st-st-stammered, hoping they'd go away and leave me alone.

It worked.

They laughed and went away.

Then Caspar the Ghost came back with a cowboy and a pirate. "Hey, you guys, this is *I don't know.*

"Think I'm kidding? Go ahead, ask him his name."

"What's your name?" the pirate asked.

I didn't say anything. I just looked away. The kids crowded around chanting, "What's your name? What's your name?"

I wanted them to leave so I blurted out, "I don't know," and they all giggled and went back to their games.

In a while, Pocahontas and Snow White came over and asked who I was. I just kept my mouth shut.

They went away probably thinking I was stupid. I didn't care.

The next day I'd be back home in Belle, West Virginia and they'd never see me again.

I wasn't mad at them or anything. I was mad at Mother for making me come to this dopey Halloween party in Aunt Betty's town.

I'd show her, I wouldn't play games, or eat ice cream, or nothing!

Two monsters came over next.
"Hey, *I don't know*, tell us your
real name." I gulped as my heart
went thumpety-thump-thump.

Frankenstein grabbed my arm and
squeezed till it hurt. "Kid, tell me
your name or I'll twist your arm
off," he threatened.

"I don't know, honest."

"Get out of here!

"You know your name. Who are
you? We've never seen you
before. Where're you from?"

"I don't know."

Lucky for me, Pastor Williams announced, "Okay, boys and girls, it's time for the contest. Remember, there's two prizes, one for best costume and one for best disguise."

Then he ordered, "Everybody line up.

"When I blow the whistle— BrreeeEEETT—like that, march up on the stage one at a time."

I jumped in between two girls in line hoping I'd be safe. I was scared-er than ever—more scared than when the old witch chased me in that creepy nightmare.

Every now and then, a kid would breakout of line, sneak up behind me and ask, "What's your name, boy? Tell us your name. Who are you?"

I wouldn't say anything, and they'd run back and get in line.

As each kid ahead of me reached center-stage, Pastor Williams asked all of us, "Okay, who is this now? Can you tell?"

Everybody yelled out the kid's name.

Nobody's costume fooled anybody.

When I finally got to center-stage, he asked, "Who is this?"

Everybody shouted, "I don't know! I don't know!"

Pastor Williams nudged me aside and told me to wait. The rest of the kids paraded across the stage as others screamed their names.

After they all passed by, the Pastor gave a prize to one kid for best costume.

Then he turned to me and said, "Looks like you've won. You fooled the kids with your disguise. I've forgotten your name. What is it again?"

I didn't say anything. He asked me again and I said, "I don't know."

He squeezed my arm—almost as hard as Frankenstein had—and whispered in my ear, "Look, I know your mother. I know your Aunt Betty. I've forgotten your first name, that's all. TELL-ME-YOUR-NAME."

He squeezed my arm again, slitted his eyes and gritted his teeth, "Come on, son, TELL ME WHO YOU ARE."

"Ned," I said, so he would let go.

He nudged me center-stage and said, "Here's Little Ned. He's the winner for best disguise. Give him a big hand."

There was noise again, kids were yelling, "No fair," and "He's not from here," and "He cheated!"

Pastor Williams handed me the prize.

I ran off the stage down a hall into a dark room and hid behind some big cardboard boxes.

I didn't move. I barely breathed. I hoped nobody would find me.

Nobody came looking for me. I stayed in my secret hiding place for a long, long time.

I swore I'd never dress up for Halloween again. I'd get sick if I had to. I'd eat worms and crickets. I'd run away from home. I'd never forgive Mother for making me come to this Halloween party in Aunt Betty's town.

I'd hate Halloween forever!

Then I heard my mother talking to Pastor Williams in the hallway. I ran to her and cried, "I wanna go home. Take me home."

"Didn't you have a good time?" Mother asked. "Pastor Williams told me you won a prize. Can I see it?"

"No! I hate Halloween! I'm never going to dress up for Halloween again.

"Please Mother, can we go back to Aunt Betty's house now?"

3. BACK TO AUNT BETTY'S HOUSE

On the way back to Aunt Betty's house Mother asked, "What do you want to be next Halloween?"

"Invisible."

✝✝ ENDING NUMBER ONE ✝✝

"I don't know."

✝✝ ENDING NUMBER TWO ✝✝

So, boys and girls, which ending
did you like the best?

The one where Little Ned says,
"Invisible."

Or, the ending where he says,
"I don't know."

Please check one:

¤ I liked the "Invisible" ending best.

¤ I liked the "I don't know" ending best.

THE OCEAN VACATION

CONTENTS

1. THE BATHTUB

More than anything in the whole wide world, I loved taking a bath.

Like I did every night, I filled the tub to the tippy top and climbed in all by myself. I splashed around, went wiggly-wiggly with my toes, held my nose under the warm soapy water, and played with my duckies and boats.

"Hurry up, Little Ned," Mother yelled from the living room. "I don't want you spending all night in the tub like you usually do.

"Daddy's got a big surprise for you."

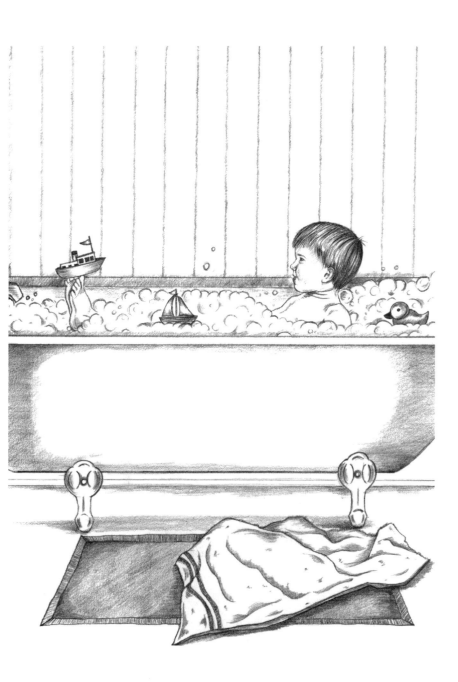

I struggled into my jammies, ran into the living room, and jumped in Daddy's lap. "What's my surprise, Daddy?"

"We're going on vacation to a place you'll really love. The Atlantic Ocean."

"Is that the big water?" I asked.

"You bet! It's bigger than a zillion bathtubs. And you can play in the ocean all day long. And you can bring your duckies and boats, too.

"First, though, Daddy's gotta teach you to swim. We'll go to the fishing lake tomorrow for your first lesson."

2. THE LAKE

The next day we drove the Chevy car to the fishing lake.

I wore my bright red swim suit Mother made for me and waded right into the shallow water all by myself.

The lake smelled funny, like Mother's garbage pail, and looked like her coffee. I couldn't see my toes like I could in the bathtub. The water was cold and tingly. I jumped up and down like a little yellow canary bird.

Then I saw them.

"Daddy, there's creepy spiders in the water," I yelled and ran up on the green grass.

"They're just little, itty-bitty spiders," Daddy said, "They won't hurt you."

"Yes, they will. They'll bite me."

"Look, they're not hurting me," he said, as he stepped into the water.

"It's cause you're bigger. They're afraid of you," I said.

"I'm...I'm little."

Mother went into the lake and beckoned me to follow. "I don't see any spiders, they're all gone. Come see."

I looked and saw spiders even though Mother didn't. I saw goopy, stringy brown stuff, too. She grabbed my arm, but I pulled away and ran back up on the green grass.

"Little Ned, I thought you liked the water," Mother said.

"Think how much you like your bath. It's even more fun in the lake. Go get your rubber duckies and come in with us."

"No! I hate spiders."

Daddy walked up on the green grass beside me and whispered, "I know a secret cove on the other side of the lake where the water is clean as spring rain. We'll go swimming there, okay?"

"Are there any spiders?"

"Nope."

"Are there slimy, dirty brown things in the water?"

"None. I swear."

We drove around the lake to the secret cove and Daddy carried me piggy-back into the lake.

Daddy held me while I splashed the water with my arms. I didn't see any spiders...or goopy stuff either.

But then I saw something slicing through the water. "Daddy, look! There's a SNAKE over there and it's coming at me."

"It won't hurt you," Daddy said. "Watch, I'll splash the water and it'll go away.

"See, it went away. It's afraid of you."

"Please take me out of the lake. I don't want the snake to bite me."

"Okay, son," Daddy sighed. "I'll just have to teach you to swim when we get to the Atlantic Ocean."

"Are there spiders and snakes in the Atlantic Ocean?"

"Don't you worry, Little Ned. It'll be fun, just you wait and see."

I sure hoped so.

I really loved the water and really wanted to swim, but not with snakes, spiders and slimy goopy things.

3. THE OCEAN

We loaded the Chevy car with
bags, towels, beach balls and pails
and headed for our ocean vacation.

As usual, I rode in the back seat so
I could sleep whenever I wanted.
Good thing, too, because the ocean
was a long, long way from home.

It took a whole day to get there.

In the morning, inside our cabin,
Mother rubbed me with sun cream,
and helped me into my bright red
bathing suit.

Then we walked down to the big
blue endless ocean.

The sun was so sparkly bright I squeezed my eyes shut. I'd never seen anything so big. The Atlantic Ocean didn't end. It just went into the sky. The ocean splashed and thundered and sounded like snoring, only louder.

As we walked, my feet sank into the hot sand. I held on tight to Mother's hand so the sand wouldn't swallow me up.

She spread a blanket and we watched the waves splash up on the beach till the sun got burny hot on my arms and back.

The next morning we walked down closer to the ocean. The sun was hot but the sand was cool next to the water.

I helped Mother gather pretty seashells.

Then I saw them. SPIDERS!

"Mother!" I yelled. "Daddy said there'd be no spiders at the ocean.

"There's lots of them jumping around, and running in and out of their holes."

My skin started to crawl like it did back at the fishing lake.

"Those aren't spiders, sweetheart, those are little crabs. They won't hurt you. Don't pay them no mind. Come on, let's walk together in the shallow water."

"I don't wanna," I said, backing away from the ocean. "There's crab-spiders in it."

"You're gonna miss a lot of fun, Little Ned. But, if you insist, we won't go in the water now.

"Go get your shovel and pail. We'll build a sand castle."

Daddy joined us and we patted sand into a big castle. Daddy knelt next to me and said, "Little Ned, YOU'VE GOT TO LEARN TO SWIM. What if you're all alone, huh? And you fall off a pier into a lake?

"You're a big boy now, six-years-old, almost seven, you can't be afraid of the water all your life."

"I'm not afraid of the water," I said to Daddy. "I just don't like creepy spiders and goopy things."

"You've got to learn to swim, and that's all there is to it." He grabbed one of my arms, Mother took the other, and together they marched me into the ocean.

"No! No! I don't want to go in the ocean," I protested loudly, but they didn't stop. The water was up to my knees and the waves were slapping my belly. I couldn't see my toes. My legs had disappeared into the water.

"Mother! Daddy! Please stop!" I begged through my tears. The water kept getting higher. My feet couldn't touch bottom anymore. The waves slapped my chin and the water tasted yucky, not like my bathwater, more like my tears.

Then I felt some thing nipping at my feet. It had to be a SNAKE!

A SNAKE! There were spiders *and* snakes in the Atlantic Ocean.

"Take me back, please," I screamed. "I hate the ocean."

But they just kept on going.

I couldn't understand why they were dragging me into the ocean. I hated turnips and they didn't make me eat them. I didn't do nothing bad.

Why did I have to be punished?

I'd show them—I'd get mad and stay mad. I wouldn't say a word. Then they'd be sorry they pulled me into the Atlantic Ocean.

When the water reached my neck, they turned around and headed back toward shore. I stopped crying, squeezed my eyes real tight, bit my lip, and hoped I'd be back on the shore real, real fast.

Back on the sand, Daddy smiled at me. "You were brave, Little Ned. You went in the ocean all the way to the deep water the very first time. I'm really proud of you. I know it was scary, but once you got the hang of it, you did real good. You'll be swimming in no time.

"I'll give you your second swimming lesson tomorrow."

He kept talking but I didn't listen. I stayed mad and didn't say anything. But I had to do something. I'd run back to the cabin and hide, then he'd be sorry.

When Daddy trotted back to the blanket to get our towels, I ran for the cabin. He shouted, but I didn't stop. I figured he'd catch me, but I didn't care. I dashed behind clumps of sea grass and between people lying on beach blankets.

I couldn't find the path to the cabin. I just kept running. I finally got tired and stopped. After I caught my breath, I looked around.

Daddy was nowhere in sight. Neither was Mother.

I was all alone.

I plopped down on the sand. Maybe they went back to the cabin to look for me.

I waited.

Maybe they were looking for me in the wrong place at the other end of the beach.

Maybe nobody came to this part of the beach cause it had dirty sand, and old, ugly logs lying around.

Maybe they were mad at me cause I didn't want to go in the ocean. Maybe they didn't care if I was lost. Maybe they were just going to leave me here all alone.

If I'd gone in the water by myself, maybe the crab-spiders wouldn't have hurt me. I coulda swatted them like flies and made them jump back in their holes.

And Daddy was right, too. I was scared on the way out to the deep water, but not on the way back. Maybe the ocean wasn't so bad after all—except for the salty, tickly taste.

Maybe I could go in the shallow water tomorrow, and learn how to swim. But where were they?

I wanted Mother and Daddy.

Then a lady said, "There, there, little boy. Why are you crying?"

"I don't know where my mother and daddy are."

"Well, let's go find them. They can't be far away."

We walked down to the edge of the ocean where the waves splashed.

The lady told big people who came by to help us find Mother and Daddy.

Soon, Mother came running and hugged me real tight for a long, long time.

"Don't you ever do that again. You scared us to death.

"We love you and we didn't mean to frighten you. You don't have to go in the Atlantic Ocean again if you don't want to.

"Just don't run away again."

Daddy arrived and squeezed us both real hard. I could hardly breathe.

"Thank goodness we found you," Daddy said. "We looked for you high and low, up and down the beach, even back at the cabin. You don't have to go in the ocean if you don't want to."

"I'll go in the ocean, I promise. Just don't leave me all alone."

"We'll never, never leave you alone again," Mother said.

"We promise."

"Daddy, will you teach me to swim in the Atlantic Ocean?"

"First thing tomorrow morning," he nodded.

"Will you teach me how to scare the crab-spiders and snakes away?"

"You bet I will."

Mother, who still held me tight, looked at me, then at Daddy and said, "I hope you don't teach him to swim too good, or it'll be just like the bathtub—I'll NEVER be able to get him out of the ocean."

Daddy laughed.

Mother laughed.

And I did, too.

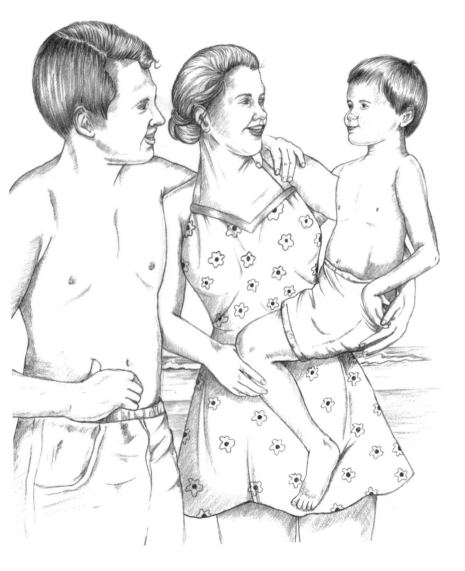

Hey, kids!

**Don't you have best friends who'd like to read
LITTLE NED STORIES?**

**Why don't you give them LITTLE NED STORIES as a
gift. That'd be awesomely cool, wouldn't it?!**

So, looky here!

**Autographed (and personalized) copies
of THE LITTLE NED STORIES—Book One can be
ordered through IM Press at the address below.**

Send a $11.00 check (includes postage and handling)
for each copy **ordered**.

IM Press
P.O. Box 5346
Takoma Park, Maryland 20913-5346

In the D.C., Maryland, Virginia area, call 301-587-1202.

Or call Book Clearing House 1-800-431-1579 to order.

And for you Internet kids, visit amazon.com, click on
children 4-8, type in LITTLE NED and order!

Hark! Teachers, Media Specialists, Museum People,
Everybody! If you'd like Edward Allan Faine to come to
your venue to show kids "How To Make A Book,"
then call 301-587-1202.